Give your child a head start with
MUPPET™ PICTURE READERS

Starring the Muppets!

Miss Piggy

Kermit

Fozzie

Dear Parent,

Now children as young as preschool age can have the fun and satisfaction of reading a book all on their own.

In every Muppet Picture Reader, there are simple words, rebus pictures, and 24 flash cards to cut out and keep. (There is a flash card for every rebus picture plus extra cards for reading practice.) After children listen to each story a couple of times, they will be ready to try it all by themselves.

Collect all the titles in our Muppet Picture Reader series. Once children have mastered these books, they can move on to Levels 1, 2, and 3 in our All Aboard Reading series.

ISBN 0-448-41551-8 A B C D E F G H I J

A MUPPET™ PICTURE READER

Miss Piggy Camps Out

Written by Lara Rice
Illustrated by Rick Brown

MUPPET PRESS
Grosset & Dunlap • New York

 was picking .

She saw

and in a .

"Yoo-hoo!" said.

"Where are you going?"

"To camp out,"

 said.

"Ooh! I love

to camp out,"

 said.

"May I come too?"

"Well...OK," 🐸 said.

So  went in

to pack her 👜.

 packed

a fancy

and fancy .

She packed a fancy

and a fancy .

She packed

a big box of  .

Soon her was full.

 put on

her dark

and her best  .

"I am ready!"

 said.

drove the

to the lake.

 pointed to a .

"That is a good spot,"

 said.

At the lake,

 and

got lots of .

 sat in the .

"It is fun to catch ,"

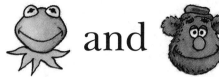 said.

Later, and

cooked out over a .

 sat on a .

"It is fun to cook out,"

 said.

The  went down.

The came out.

 put up

their  .

"It is time to sleep.

, where is

your ?" said.

"  ?"  said.

"I do not have a  !

I do not want a  !

I want a  !

A fancy  !"

 said.

And she called a  .

 got in

the 🚕.

The 🚕

took 🐷

to a hotel.

"It is fun to camp out,"  said.

flowers	Miss Piggy
Fozzie	Kermit
bag	car

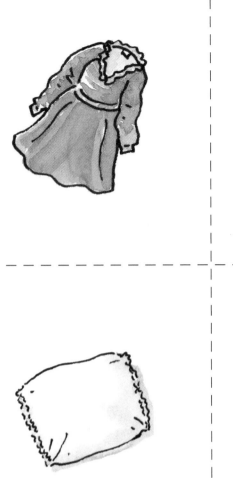

gloves	dress
fan	pillow
glasses	candy

tree

hat

boat

fish

rock

fire

stars	sun
bed	tent
book	taxi